W. R. Nicoll

Songs of Rest

W. R. Nicoll

Songs of Rest

ISBN/EAN: 9783337019877

Printed in Europe, USA, Canada, Australia, Japan

Cover: Foto ©Andreas Hilbeck / pixelio.de

More available books at **www.hansebooks.com**

Songs of Rest.

EDITED BY

Sir W. R. NICOLL, M.A.

"And Moses drew near unto the thick darkness
where God was."

New York:

JAMES POTT, 12 ASTOR PLACE.

Thanks are due Messrs. Houghton, Mifflin, & Co., for permission to use several Copyright Poems.

James Pott.

New York, Oct. 1882.

CONTENTS.

5.—The Aged and the Dying.

Desponding Believers.

"Thus saith the high and lofty One that inhabiteth eternity, whose name is Holy; I dwell in the high and holy place, with him also that is of a contrite and humble spirit, to revive the spirit of the humble, and to cheer the heart of the contrite one."—*Isaiah* lvii. 15.

"I believe in the forgiveness of sins."—*The Apostles' Creed.*

"The faintest longing to love *is* love; the very dread to miss for ever the face of God is love; the very terror at that dreadful state where none can love is love."—*E. B. Pusey, D.D.*

Why art thou Sorrowful?

HY art thou sorrowful, servant of God?
    And what is this dulness that hangs o'er
      thee now?
Sing the praises of Jesus, and sing them aloud,
And the song shall dispel the dark cloud from thy
    brow.

For is there a thought in the wide world so sweet
As that God has so cared for us, bad as we are,
That He thinks of us, plans for us, stoops to entreat,
And follows us, wander we ever so far?

Then how can the heart e'er be drooping or sad
Which God hath once touched with the light of His
     grace?
Can the child have a doubt who but lately hath laid
Himself to repose in his Father's embrace?

And is it not wonderful, servant of God!
That He should have honoured us so with His love
That the sorrows of life should but shorten the road
Which leads to Himself and the mansion above?

Oh then, when the spirit of darkness comes down
With clouds and uncertainties into thy heart,
One look to the Saviour, one thought of thy crown
And the tempest is over, the shadows depart.

That God hath once whispered a word in thine ear,
Or sent thee from heaven one sorrow for sin,
Is enough for a life both to banish all fear,
And to turn into peace all the troubles within.

Then why dost thou weep so? For see how time
flies—
The time that for loving and praising was given.
Away with thee, child; then, and hide thy red eyes
In the lap, the kind lap, of thy Father in heaven.

F. W. Faber.

Resting in God's Love.

O Lord, how happy is the time
   When in Thy love I rest!
When from my weariness I climb
   Even to Thy tender breast!
The night of sorrow endeth there—
   Thou art brighter than the sun:
And in Thy pardon and Thy care
   The heaven of heavens is won.

Let the world call herself my foe,
   Or let the world allure;
I care not for the world—I go
   To this dear Friend and sure.
And when life's fiercest storms are sent
   Upon life's wildest sea,
My little bark is confident,
   Because it holds by Thee.

When the law threatens endless death
   Upon the awful hill,
Straightway from her consuming breath
   My soul goes higher still:—
Goeth to Jesus wounded, slain,
   And maketh him her home,
Whence she will not go out again,
   And where death cannot come.

A 3

I do not fear the wilderness
  Where Thou hast been before,
Nay rather will I daily press
  After Thee, hear Thee more.
Thou art my food ; on Thee I lean ;
  Thou makest my heart sing ;
And to Thy heavenly pastures green
  All Thy dear flock dost bring.

And if the gate that opens there
  Be dark to other men,
It is not dark to those who share
  The heart of Jesus then.
That is not losing much of life,
  Which is not losing Thee,
Who art as present in the strife
  As in the victory.

Therefore how happy is the time
  When in Thy love I rest !
When from my weariness I climb
  Even to Thy tender breast !
The night of sorrow endeth there- -
  Thou art brighter than the
And in Thy pardon and Thy
  The heaven of heavens is won

Translated by George Mac Donald.

To a Mourner.

Do you know what you are saying?
  All the days are dark to you—
Never comes a lift or lightening—
  Never strength to smile them through!

Do you know that every life-time,
  Yes, the narrowest and most drear,
Is a cup that still runs over
  With the gifts of God most dear?

Do you know that thousands, thousands,
  In this world of sin and shame,
Bear a burden to which yours is
  But the emptiest, idlest name?

Do you know God's saints are chosen
  Oftentimes to suffer sore,
That the crown may be more golden,
  When the suffering is o'er?

Do you know He gives them sorrow,
  Makes it often sharp and long,
That their voices may be sweeter
  When they join the glad " New Song."

Do you know the lot He chose Him,
  When on earth He drew His breath.

Was the cradle in the manger,—
　And the house at Nazareth?

Do you know the path He travell'd
　Firmly, strongly, day by day—
How the thorns and tears commingled,
　Till the cross barr'd up the way?

Do you know how dark the death-cave—
　How she wept there, Magdalene;
Soon how real the Resurrection,
　And the great Ascension Scene?

Yes, you know it, dry your tears then;
　Cease your mourning; change your ways,
Look for God's high forward meanings;
　His the power and His the praise.

Alfred Norris.

A Call to Wandering Children.

My blood so red
For thee was shed,
Come home again, come home again,
   My own sweet heart, come home again.
You've gone astray
Out of your way,
Come home again, come home again.
> *From a MS. of the 17th Century, quoted
> by Charles Stanford, D.D.*

The City of Rest.

O birds from out the east, O birds from out the west,
Have you found that happy city in all your weary
quest?
Tell me, tell me, from earth's wanderings may the
heart find glad surcease,
Can ye show me, as an earnest, any olive branch of
peace?
I am weary of life's troubles, of its sin and toil and
care,
I am faithless, crushing in my heart so many a
fruitless prayer,
O birds from out the east, O birds from out the west,
Can ye tell me of that city, the name of which is
Rest?

O little birds fly east again—O little birds fly west:
Ye have found no happy city in all your weary quest,
Still shall ye find no spot of rest wherever ye may
stray,
And still like you the human soul must wing its
weary way,
There sleepeth no such city within the wide world's
bound,
Nor hath the dreaming fancy yet its blissful
portals found:
We are but children crying here upon a mother's
breast,
For life and peace and blessedness, and for eternal
Rest.

Bless God, I hear a still small voice above life's
    clamorous din,
Saying, "Faint not, O weary one, thou yet may'st
    enter in,
That city is prepared for those who well do win the
    fight,
Who tread the winepress till its blood hath washed
    their garments white,
Within it is no darkness, nor any baleful flower
Shall there oppress thy weeping eyes with stupefy-
    ing power,
It lieth calm within the light of God's peace-giving
    breast,
Its walls are called Salvation, the city's name is
    Rest."

Anon.

The Day is Over.

The day is over,
  The feverish careful day;
Can I recover
  Strength that has ebbed away?
Can ever sleep such freshness give,
That I again should wish to live?

Let me lie down,
  No more I seek to have
A heavenly crown:
  Give me a quiet grave,
Release, and not reward, I ask,-
Too hard for me life's heavy task.

Now let me rest:
  Hushed be my striving brain,
My beating breast ;
  Let me put off my pain,
And feel me sinking, sinking deep
Into an abyss of sleep.

The morrow's noise,
  Its anguish, hope and fear,
Its empty joys,
  Of these I shall not hear:
Call me no more, I cannot come
I'm gone to be at rest at home.

Earth undesired
   And not for heaven meet,
In one so tired
   What's left but slumber sweet—
Beneath a grassy mound of trees,
Or at the bottom of the seas?

   Yet let me have
      Once in a thousand years
   Thoughts in my grave;
      To know how free from fears
I sleep, and that I there shall lie
Through undisturbed eternity.

   And when I wake
      Then let me hear above
   The birds that make
      Songs, not of human love:
Or muffled tones my ear may reach
Of storms that sound from beach to beach.

   But hark! what word
      Breathes through the twilight dim?
   " Rest in the Lord,
      Wait patiently for him.
Return, O soul, and thou shalt have
A better rest than in thy grave."

   My God, I come;
      But I was sorely shaken;
   Art Thou my home?
      thought I was forsaken:
I know Thou art a sweeter rest
Than earth's soft side, or ocean's breast.

Yet this my cry:
  "I ask no more for heaven;
Now let me die,
  For I have vainly striven!"
I had but for that word from Thee
Renounced my immortality.

Now I return,
  Return, O Lord, to me,
I cannot earn
  That heaven I'll ask of Thee.
But with Thy peace amid the strife
I still can live in hope of life.

The careful day,
  The feverish day is over;
Strength ebbed away,
  I lie down to recover;
I sleep with Him, I shall be blest,
Whose word has brought my sorrows rest.

T. T. Lynch.

Forsaken.

Martyrs, through fire and steel,
Have felt the tracking of the steadfast eye,
Of faithful friend or kind disciple nigh,
That strengthened them; beside the cruel wheel
Hath woman waited, wiping from a face,
Beloved, the damps of anguish; Kings in chase,
Upon the mountains held from day to day,
Have leaned on peasants scorning to betray.
The baffled hope, the discrownèd: nay,
A hand unseen upon a tyrant's tomb,
Hath scatter'd flowers; so strong above disgrace,
Despair and death, rise human hearts; of whom—
King, Martyrs, Malefactors—it is said
That all forsook Him, all forsook and fled,
Save of one only! Human love forsakes,
Yet is not all forsaken! He that takes
This drear pre-eminence of woe alone,
Forsaketh never, never! He hath known
That pang too well; O Saviour with Thine own.
Too little seemed it for Thy love to share
All bitter draughts, so hast Thou bid this cup
Pass from our souls for ever, drinking up
Its wormwood and its gall, our lips to spare.
                              Dora Greenwell.

The Anxious

ABOUT THEIR FUTURE — ABOUT GOD'S
PROVIDENCE — ABOUT THEIR FRIENDS.

"Thou hast given us Thine own Son, and wilt Thou no give us bread?"—*William Anderson, LL D.*

"He shall bring forth the headstone with shoutings."—*Zech.* iv. 7.

"And he said unto Jesus, Lord, remember me when thou comest into thy kingdom. And Jesus said unto him, Verily I say unto thee, To-day shal thou be with me in paradise."—*Luke* xxiii. 4?, 43.

Consider the Ravens.

ORD, according to Thy words,
I have considered Thy birds;
And I find their life good,
And better the better understood:
Sowing neither corn nor wheat,
They have all that they can eat.

Reaping no more than they sow,
They have all they can stow;
Having neither barn nor store,
Hungry again, they eat more.

Considering, I see, too, that they
Have a busy life, and plenty of play:
In the earth they dig their bills deep,
And work well though they do not heap:
Then to play in the air they are not loath,
And their nests between are better than both.

But this is when there blow no storms;
When berries are plenty in winter, and worms;
When their feathers are thick, and oil is enough
To keep the cold out and the rain off:
If there should come a long hard frost,
Then it looks as if Thy birds were lost.

But I consider further, and find
A hungry bird has a free mind ;
He is hungry to-day, not to-morrow:
Steals no comfort, no grief doth borrow:
This moment is his, Thy will hath said it,
The next is nothing till Thou hast made it.

The bird has pain, but has no fear,
Which is the worst of any gear :
When cold and hunger and harm betide him
He gathers them not to stuff inside him:
Content with the day's ill he has got,
He waits just nor haggles with his lot :
Neither jumbles God's will
With dribblets from his own still.

But next I see, in my endeavour.
Thy birds here do not live for ever :
That cold or hunger, sickness or age,
Finishes their earthly stage;
The rook drops without a stroke,
And never gives another croak ;
Birds lie here, and birds lie there,
With little feathers all astare:
And in Thy own sermon, Thou
That the sparrow falls dost allow.

It shall not cause me any alarm,
For neither so comes the bird to harm,
Seeing our Father, Thou hast said,
Is by the sparrow's dying bed:

Therefore it is a blessed place,
And the sparrow in high grace,
It cometh, therefore, to this, Lord:
I have considered Thy word,
And henceforth will be Thy Bird.

George Mac Donald.

"The Sunrise never failed us yet."

Upon the sadness of the sea
The sunset broods regretfully,
From the far lonely spaces slow
Withdraws the wistful after glow.

So out of life the splendour dies,
So darken all the happy skies,
So gathers twilight, cold and stern,
But overhead the planets burn.

And up the east another day,
Shall chase the bitter dawn away,
What though our eyes with tears be wet!
The sunrise never failed us yet.

The blush of dawn may yet restore
Our light, and hope and joy once more,
Sad soul take comfort, nor forget
That sunrise never failed us yet.

Celia Thaxte

Christmas Bells.

It chanced upon the merry, merry Christmas Eve,
I went singing past the church, across the moorland dreary,
Oh! never sin, and want, and woe, this earth will
leave,
And the bells but mark the wailing sound, they sing
so cheery.

How long, O Lord! how long before Thou come
again?
Still in cellar, and in garret, and on moorland dreary
The orphans moan, and widows weep, and poor men
toil in vain,
Till the earth is sick of hope deferred, though
Christmas bells be cheery.

Then arose a joyous clamour from the wild fowl on
the mere,
Beneath the stars, across the snow, like clear bells
ringing ;
And a voice within cried, Listen! Christmas carols
even here !
Though thou be dumb ; yet o'er their work the stars
and snows are singing.

Blind! I live, I love, I reign; and all the nations
    through,
With the thunder of my judgments even now are
    ringing,
Do thou fulfil thy work, but as yon wild-fowl do,
Thou wilt heed no less the wailing, yet hear through
    it the angels singing

Charles Kingsley.

The Mystery of God's Providence.

You hear an endless cry that goes
   Lamenting through the sombre air,
Of nations bent with many woes,
   Or gauntly wrestling with despair.
I hear a psalm by myriads sung—
   A psalm that knows no stint nor stay,
And lo! a voice calls old and young
   To be indeed as blest as they.

You watch a life bereft of light,
   For ever wrapt in unthinned gloom,
Whose only tranquil time seems night,
   Whose happiest hope and rest the tomb;
I watch the life and know that God
   So guides the soul to heaven above,
You only see the smiting rod—
   But ah! the Power that smites is Love.

You see a world that wildly whirls
   Through coiling clouds of battle smoke,
And drench'd with blood the children's curls,
   And women's hearts by thousands broke,
I see a host above it all,
   Where angels wield their conquering sword,
And thrones may rise or thrones may fall,
   But comes the kingdom of the Lord.
                   Alfred Norris.

C

"Not Without Hope."

They say you are not as you were,
　In days of long ago ;
That clouds came o'er your sun at noon,
　And dimmed its golden glow.

Yet every gentler word I say,
　Each gentler deed I do,
Is but a blossom on the grave,
　Where sleeps my love for you.

And can a weed bring forth a flower?
　Or blight bear beauty? Nay,
This darkness is but short eclipse,
　To surely pass away.

Though one by one my early friends
　Have faded from my prayer,
Your name was always first and last,
　And still it lingers there.

I love but dearer for my fears,
　And prayers for such an one,
I think God does not love us less
　For costing Him His Son.

And I believe when death shall break
　This spell of human pain,
The love that I to God entrust
　He'll give to me again.

Isabella Fyvie Mayo.

The Father of the Fatherless.

DORSET DIALECT.

As I wer readèn ov a stwone,
In Grenley Church-yard, all alwone.
A little maid ran up, wi' pride,
To zee me there ; an' push'd aside
A bunch o' bennets, that did hide
A verse, her father, as she zaid
Put up above her mother's head,
To tell how much he loved her.

The verse wer short, but very good,
I stood and learn'd en where I stood,
" Mid God, dear Mary, gie me greäce,
To vind, like thee, a better pleace,
Where I, oonce mwore, mid zee thy feäce,
An' bring thy children up, to know
His word, that they mid come and show
Thy soul how much I loved thee."

"Where's father, then," I zaid, "my chile?"
"Dead too," she answer'd wi' a smile:
"An' I an' brother Jem do bide
At Betty White's, o' tother zide
O' road."—"Mid He, my chile," I cried.
"That's father to the fatherless,
Become thy father now, an' bless,
An' keep, an' lead, an' love thee."

Though she've a' lost, I thought, so much,
Still He don't let the thoughts o't touch
Her litsome heart, by day or night ;
An' zoo, if we could teäke it right,
Do show He'll meäke his burdens light
To weaker souls ; and that His smile
Is sweet upon a little chile,
When they be dead that loved it.

W. Barnes.

Defeated.

My darling, O my darling! with the soft sad eyes,
Set like twilight planets in the raining skies,
With the brow all patience and the lips all pain,
Save the curve for kisses—kiss me, love, once again.

My priestess, O my priestess! with the almond
    bough
That her pale hand holdeth, dry and barren now,
With its crown of blossoms by the rude wind rent,
With the gift God-taken that of God was sent.

Mine empress, O mine empress! with the shatter'd
    throne,
Is there yet no kingdom we can call thine own?
Is success the only thing the world holds good?
Or is God as man, and could not, if He would?

No, no, by all the martyrs, and the dear dead
    Christ;
By the long bright roll of those whom joy enticed,
With her myriad blandishments, but could not win,
Who would fight for victory, but would not sin.

By these, our elder brothers, who have gone before,
And have left their trail of light upon our shore.
We can see the glory of a seeming shame,
We can feel the fulness of an empty name.

                  Sarah Williams.

Against Tears.

The world is all too sad for tears,
  I would not weep, not I,
But smile along my life's short road,
  Until I, smiling, die.

The little flowers breathe sweetness out.
  Through all the dewy night;
Shall I more churlish be than they,
  And plain for constant light?

Not so, not so, no load of woe
  Need bring despairing frown;
For while we bear it, we can bear,
  Past that, we lay it down.

                    Sarah Williams.

Come unto Me.

Heart-broken and weary, where'er thou mayst be,
There are no words like these words for comforting
   thee;
When sorrows come round thee like waves of the
   sea,
The Saviour says cheerfully, "Come unto Me."

There are no words like these words, "Come hither
   and rest,"
Afflicted, forsaken, the thorn in thy breast
All lonely and helpless He thought upon thee,
And He said in His tenderness, "Come unto Me."

O Saviour! my spirit would fain be at rest:
There are passions which rage like a storm in my
   breast,
O show me the road along which I must flee,
And strengthen me, Saviour, to come unto Thee.

There are no words like these words: how blessed
   they be,
How calming when Jesus says, "Come unto Me!"
O hear them, my heart, they were spoken to thee,
And still they are calling thee, "Come unto Me."

I will walk through the world with these words on
    my heart,
Through sorrow or sin they shall never depart,
And, when dying, I hope He will whisper to me.
" I have loved thee, and saved thee ; come, sinner.
    to Me."

Edwin Paxton Hood.

The Sick and the Maimed.

" He whom thou lovest is sick."—*John* xi. 3.

" Indeed he was sick."—*Phil.* ii. 27.

"It is better for thee to enter into life halt or maimed, rather than having two hands or two feet to be cast into everlasting fire."—*Matt.* xviii. 8.

A Reverie in Sickness.

 FANCY I hear a whisper,
As of leaves in a gentle air;
Is it wrong, I wonder, to fancy
It may be the tree up there?
The tree that heals the nations,
Growing amidst the street,
And dropping for who will gather
Its apples at their feet.

I fancy I hear a rushing
As of waters down a slope ;
Is it wrong, I wonder, to fancy,
It may be the river of hope
The river of crystal waters,
That flows from the very throne
And runs through the street of the city.
With a softly jubilant tone.

I fancy a twilight round me,
And a wandering of the breeze,
With a hush in that high city,
And a going in the trees.
But I know there will be no night there,
No coming and going day,
For the holy face of the Father
Will be perfect light alway.

I could do without the darkness
And better without the sun;
But oh! I should like a twilight,
After the day was done!
Would He lay His hand on His forehead,
On His hair as white as wool,
And shine one hour through His fingers.
Till the shadow had made me cool.

But the thought is very foolish:
If that face I did but see,
All else would be all forgotten --
River, and twilight, and tree;
I should seek, I should care for nothing,
Beholding His countenance;
And fear only to lose one glimmer
By one single sideway glance.

'Tis again but a foolish fancy,
To picture the countenance so,
Which is shining in all our spirits
Making them white as snow,
Come to me, shine in me, Master.
And I care not for river or tree,
Care for no sorrow or crying
If only Thou shine in me.

I would lie on my bed for ages,
Looking out on the dusty street,
Where whisper, nor leaves, nor waters.
Nor anything cool and sweet.
At my heart this ghastly fainting,
And this burning in my blood,
If only I knew thou wast with me.
Wast with me and making me good.

George Mac Donald.

"Complete in Him."

Dear Lord, it is better that I
Should go through the world with one eye,
If Thou, Light and Guide, be but nigh.

It is better, O Saviour divine,
To lose this right hand of mine,
If Thou hold but the other in Thine.

Thou only canst make me complete;
And to limp by Thy side were more sweet,
Than walking alone on both feet.

Joseph A. Torrey.

D

Born Blind.

"WHEREAS I WAS BLIND, NOW I SEE."—JOHN ix. 25

That summer morn you stood where thick
   The clustering roses burned;
And though your face was sweet with peace,
   From meek submission learned,
Through the closed curtains of your eyes,
   The soul looked out and yearned.

It was a weary journey, dear,
   Of which you tired so soon—
You never saw the glad green earth
   At peace in summer's noon,
Nor ever knew how ocean moans,
   And foams beneath the moon.

But if you never saw our joys,
   You never saw our sin,
Our faces worn with tracks of tears,
   And warring thoughts within,
Our eyes that strain with longing for
   The peace they cannot win.

You saw your loved ones first in heaven,
   With its deep peace in their eyes.
You saw the new Jerusalem
   'Neath unpolluted skies,
And all things glad in God's clear light.
   And love's sweet harmonies.

No night. no storm, come in these fair
  Eternal years to mar
The glory near and clear you see.
  To us so dimmed and far.
And Jesus as He is—your Sun,
  Who is our morning Star.

W. R. N.

The Angel of Patience.

To weary hearts, to mourning homes
God's meekest angel gently comes:
No power has he to banish pain,
Or give us back our lost again.
And yet in tenderest love our dear
And heavenly Father sends him here.

There's quiet in that angel's glance,
There's rest in his still countenance !
He mocks no grief with idle cheer,
Nor wounds with words the mourner's ear;
But ills and woes He may not cure.
He kindly trains us to endure.

Angel of Patience ! sent to calm
Our feverish brows with cooling palm:
To lay the storms of hope and fear,
And reconcile life's smile and tear:
The throbs of wandering pride to still,
And make our own our Father's will !

O thou who mournest on the way,
With longings for the close of day:
He walks with thee, that Angel kind,
And gently whispers " Be resigned ; "
Bear up, bear on, the end shall tell,
The dear Lord ordereth all things well !

J. G. Whittier.

The Bereaved.

" I shall clasp thee again, O soul of my soul,
And with God be the rest."

Robert Browning.

Our Angel Child.

ALWAYS lightest was her laughter,
  There was dream-land in its tone
  Though she mingled with the children,
Yet she always seem'd alone.
And her prattle—'Twas but child's talk—
  Yet it always sparkled o'er
With a strange and shadowy wisdom,
  With a bird-like, fairy lore,
Which you could not help but fancy
  You had somewhere heard before,
In some old-world happy version,
  By a bright Elysian shore.

All the little children loved her—
  None so joyous in their play:
And yet ever there was something
  Which seem'd—Ah! so far away,
For the joyance and the laughter,
  And the streamlet's crisping foam—
'Twas as if some little song-bird
  Had dropp'd down from yon blue dome;
Warbling still among the others,
  Wandering with them where they roam,
And yet hallowing remembrance
  With low gushes about home!

Oh the glory of those child eyes!
    Oh the music of her feet!
Oh those peals of spirit laughter
    Coming up the village street!
Shall we never hear her knocking
    At the little ivied door?
Will she never run to kiss us
    Bounding o'er the oaken floor?
Has that music gone for ever?
    Are those tender lispings o'er?
Oh the terror! Oh the anguish,
    Of that one word—evermore!

Ever was she but a stranger
    Among the sublunary things:
All her life was but the folding
    Of her gorgeous spirit-wings—
Nothing more than a forgetting—
    Still she gave more than she took
From the sunlight or the starlight,
    From the meadow or the brook:—
There was music in her silence,
    There was wisdom in her look:
There was raying out of beauty
    As from some transcendent book:
She was wonderful as grottoes
    With strange gods in every nook!

And at night amid the silence,
    With the little prayer-clasped hands,
She look'd holy as the Christ-Church
    Rising white in Pagan lands:

Seem'd she but the faltering prelude,
  To a great tale of God's throne—
As a flower dropp'd out of heaven,
  Telling whither it has grown.
But she left us—she our angel—
  Without murmur, without moan,
And we woke and found it starlight—
  Found that we were all alone,
And as desolate as birds' nests
  When the fledglings all have flown !

Bu our house has been made sacred—
  Sacred every spot she trod;
For she came a starry preacher,
  Dedicating all to God.
Render thanks unto the Giver,
  Though his gift be out of sight,
For a jubilant to-morrow,
  Shall come after this to-night.
She hath left a spirit glory
  Blending with the grosser light,
Oh the earth to us is holy !
  Oh the other world is bright !

John Stanyan Bigg.

"For of Such is the Kingdom."

Just opened blue eyes, and looked on the world,
    then made no further stay,
When you put your darling in my arms I hadn't a
    word to say,
And through my tears came the blinding thought,
    "God's way is a terrible way,
I couldn't have dealt to my foe the stroke He has
    dealt to His own to-day."

Such a tiny, precious thing. just made for a
    mother's love to enfold,
The little feet too feeble yet to tread the streets of
    gold,
The howling winds were wild without, and dank
    rains drenched the mould,
It was hard to lay the helpless babe out in the storm
    and cold.

I know in love our Master took your darling little
    lad ;
Some say, "The baby-head is crowned and the
    baby-heart is glad,
He might have lived a godless life—now wherefore
    go so sad?
It was in mercy that our Lord took from you all
    you had."

Does God snatch souls away from life lest they
    stumble in the race !
Nay, verily, His chosen ones only behold His face;
Living or dying, in God's heaven your babe had
    found a place,
Purer than earth his new-born soul went straight to
    Christ's embrace.

I think he'll learn to know you there, in child
    accents lisp your name,
Do heaven's great harmonies of love shut out a
    parent's claim ?
The passionate heart of motherhood woke in you
    when he came,
And, one day, dear love answering yours will satisfy
    the flame.

Ah friend ! we sinful struggling souls need a close
    human tie;
Need heart of heart, and life of life to draw us to
    the sky,
When the hands of earth grow slack, the soul goes
    out in a great cry
That is only stilled in the echo of the new song sung
    on high.

We hear the breaking billows as all doubting here
    we stand ;
We cannot see the glory and green verdure of that
    strand ;
But we put fair flowers of hawthorn in the tiny
    waxen hand,
And say, " Our darling wakens in a better, brighter
    land."   *Eliza W. Nicoll.*

" When the Night and Morning Meet."

In the dark and narrow street,
  Into a world of woe,
Where the tread of many feet
  Went trampling to and fro,
A child was born (speak low),
  When the night and morning meet.

Full seventy summers back,
  Was this—so long ago,
The feet that wore the track,
  Are lying straight and low.
Yet there hath been no lack
  Of passers to and fro.

Within the narrow street
  This Childhood ever played;
Beyond this narrow street,
  This Manhood never strayed:
This age sat still and prayed,
  Anear the trampling feet.

The tread of ceaseless feet
  Flowed through his life, unstirred
By waters fall, or fleet
  Wind music, or the bird
Of morn, these sounds are sweet,
  But they were still unheard.

Within the narrow street
  I stood beside a bed,
I held a dying head,
  When the night and morning meet.
And every word was sweet,
  Though few the words we said.

And as we spoke, dawn drew
  To day—the world was fair
In fields afar I knew,
  Yet spoke not to him there,
Of how the grasses grew,
  Besprent with dew-drops rare.

We spoke not of the sun,
  Nor of this green earth fair,
This Soul, whose day was done,
  Had never claimed its share
In these, and yet its rare,
  Rich heritage had won.

From the dark and narrow street,
  Into a world of love,
A child was born, speak low,
  Speak reverent; for we know
Not how they meet above,
  When the night and morning meet.

Dora Greenwell.

E

Released.

A little low-ceiled room.   Four walls
   Whose blank shut out all else of life.
And crowded close within their bound,
   A world of pain, and toil, and strife.

Her world.   Scarce furthermore she knew
   Of God's great globe that wondrously
Outrolls a glory of green earth,
   And frames it with the restless sea.

Four closer walls of common pine
   And therein lieth, cold and still,
The weary flesh that long hath borne
   Its patient mystery of ill.

Regardless now of work to do:
   No queen more careless in her state;
Hands crossed in their unbroken calm
   For other hands the work must wait.

Put by her implements of toil,
   Put by each coarse intrusive sign,
She made a Sabbath when she died,
   And round her breathes a Rest Divine.

Put by at last beneath the lid,
  The exempted hands, the tranquil face:
Uplift her in her dreamless sleep,
  And bear her gently from the place.

Oft she hath gazed with wistful eyes,
  Out on that threshold from the night:
The narrow bourne she crosseth now,
  She standeth in the Eternal Light.

Oft she hath pressed with aching feet
  Those broken steps that reach the door.
Henceforth with angels she shall tread
  Heaven's golden stair for evermore.

A. D. T. Whitney

"As in a Glass Darkly."

Ah well, shall I wonder you left me!
  That World is a rest:
For so it is written. But this one,
  A battle at best.
Where the victors have scant time for wearing
  The green laurel crown,
And the vanquish'd go down like the dry leaves,
  When woodlands are brown.

You were young. You were gentle. You waited
  With sorrowful eyes,
As vanished in fleeting succession,
  Rich prize after prize.
Till at last your small hands were left empty,
  And, tired of the strife,
You turn'd to the Master. He led you
  Away into life.

It is long since I saw you. I weary
  And thirst every day,
Every day!—every hour I ponder,
  All wistful the way,
That leads to the kingdom you dwell in,
  You trod it full fast,
But I caught—was it only a fancy?—
  One sigh as you pass'd.

Shall I meet you some day with the angels,
  Your beauty all new?
Will your soft eyes look on me so fondly,
  As they used to do,
When you gather'd my head to your bosom,
  With tender caress,
And my lips with a sweet touch of welcome,
  You bent down to press!

I hope for such meeting—I lost you
  So much left untold!
But perhaps even now you know all things,
  The new and the old;
Perhaps even now you are nearer
  Than ever before,
And you smile as you watch me come to you,
  A Lost Love no more!

            Alfred Norris.

Vesta.

O Christ of God! whose life and death,
  Our own have reconciled,
Most quietly, most tenderly
  Take home Thy star-named child!

Thy grace is in her patient eyes,
  Thy words are on her tongue:
The very silence round her seems
  As if the angels sung.

Her smile is as a listening child's
  Who hears its mother call;
The lilies of Thy perfect peace,
  About her pillow fall.

She leans from out our clinging arms,
  To rest herself in Thine;
Alone to Thee, dear Lord, can we
  Our well-beloved resign!

O, less for her than for ourselves,
  We bow our heads and pray;
Her setting star, like Bethlehem's.
  To thee shall point the way!

                    J. G. Whittier.

The E'en brings a' Hame

Upon the hills the wind is sharp and cold,
The sweet young grasses wither on the wold,
And we, O Lord, have wandered from Thy fold,
   But evening brings us home.

Among the mists we stumbled and the rocks,
Where the brown lichen whitens and the fox
Watches the straggler from the scattered flocks,
   But evening brings us home.

The sharp thorns prick us, and our tender feet
Are cut and bleeding, and the lambs repeat
Their pitiful complaints—oh rest is sweet,
   When evening brings us home.

We have been wounded by the hunter's darts,
Our eyes are very heavy, and our hearts
Search for Thy coming, when the light departs,
   At evening bring us home.

The darkness gathers, thro' the gloom no star
Rises to guide. We have wandered far,
Without Thy lamp we know not where we are,
   At evening bring us home.

The clouds are round us and the snow drifts thicken.
O Thou dear shepherd leave us not to sicken.
In the waste night, our tardy footsteps quicken.
  At evening bring us home.

Shirley.

Bereavement.

When some Beloveds 'neath whose eyelids lay
The sweet lights of my childhood, one by one,
Did leave me dark, before the natural sun,
And I astonied fell and could not pray,—
A thought within me to myself did say,
" Is God less God that *thou* art left undone ?
Rise, worship, bless Him, in this sackcloth spun,
As in that purple !"—But I answered, Nay !
What child his filial heart in words can loose,
If he beheld his tender father raise
The hand that chastens sorely ? can he choose
But sob in silence with an upward gaze ?
And *my* great Father, thinking fit to bruise,
Discerns in speechless tears both prayer and praise.

E. B. Browning.

Consolation.

All are not taken: there are left behind
Living Beloveds, tender looks to bring
And make the daylight still a happy thing,
And tender voices, to make soft the wind,
But if it were not so—if I could find
No love in all the world for comforting,
Nor any path but hollowly did ring,
Where "dust to dust" the love from life disjoined,
And if, before those sepulchres unmoving
I stood alone (as some forsaken lamb
Goes bleating up the moors in weary dearth)
Crying, "Where are you, O my loved and loving."
I know a Voice would sound, "Daughter," I Am:
Can I suffice for Heaven and not for earth.

E. B. Browning

In Time of Trouble.

Rejoice when thou dost see
God take thy things from thee;
  Ay—the greater the loss,
  And the heavier the cross
  The greater the gain shall be,
When thy props are laid low,
And friend turns to foe,
  'Tis but because now
  God seeth that thou
No longer on crutches must go—
    Each here
  Whom he setteth alone,
  He Himself is most near.

Bjornsterne Bjernsen.*

* From " Fells and Fiords of Norway."

The Sleep.

"HE GIVETH HIS BELOVED SLEEP."

Of all the thoughts of God that are
Borne inward into souls afar,
Along the Psalmist's music deep,
Now tell me if that any is,
For gift or grace surpassing this—
"He giveth His belovëd, sleep?"

What would we give to our belovèd?
The hero's heart to be unmoved,
The poet's star-tuned harp to sweep,
The patriot's voice to teach and rouse,
The monarch's crown to light the brows?
" He giveth His belovëd, sleep."

What do we give to our beloved?
A little faith all undisproved,
A little dust to overweep,
And bitter memories to make
The whole world blasted for our sake:
"He giveth His belovëd, sleep."

Sleep soft, beloved ! we sometimes say,
Who have no tune to charm away
Sad dreams that through the eyelids creep:
But never doleful dream again,
Shall break the happy slumber when
" He giveth His belovëd, sleep."

O earth so full of dreary noises!
O men with wailing in your voices !
O delvèd gold the wailers heap!
O strife, O curse, that o'er it fall !
God strikes a silence through you all,
" And giveth His belovëd, sleep."

His dews drop mutely on the hill,
His cloud above it saileth still,
Though on its slope men sow and reap:
More softly than the dew is shed,
Or cloud is floated overhead,
" He giveth His belovëd, sleep."

Ay, men may wonder when they scan
A living, thinking, feeling man,
Confirmed in such a rest to keep;
But angels say, and through the word
I think their happy smile is heard—
" He giveth His belovëd, sleep."

For me, my heart that erst did go
Most like a tired child at a show,
That sees through tears the mummers leap,
Would now its wearied vision close,
Would, childlike, on His love repose,
" Who giveth His belovëd, sleep."

And friends, dear friends, when it shall be
That this low breath is gone from me,
And round my bier ye come to weep,
Let one, most loving of you all,
Say, not a tear must o'er her fall,
He giveth His belovëd, sleep."

E. B. Browning.

F

A Dirge.

Low you lie, my dear,
      In the grave;
Tall grass over you
Mix'd with violet blue,
Primrose, daisy, too:
      Low you lie.

Sound you sleep, my dear,
      In the grave.
Clouds their thunder throw,
Loud winds hoarsely blow,
Drifts the sleet and snow.
      Sound you sleep.

Long you stay, my dear,
      In the grave;
Sunshine falls about,
Birds from nests peep out,
Children sing and shout.
      Long you stay

You will rise, my dear,
      From the grave.
All your being stirred
By a spoken word,
Oh, so gladly heard!
      You will rise.

Alfred Norris.

The Remainder.

Lord, what remains;
When I would count my gains,
I find that Thou hast torn them all away;
  And under summer suns I shrink with cold,
  Shiver, and faint with hunger, yet behold
My brethren strong and satisfied and gay.

  I had a friend
  Whose love no time could end:
That friend didst Thou to Thine own bosom take
  For this my loss I see no reparation:
  The earth was once my home: a habitation
Of sorrow hast Thou made it for this sake.

  I had a dream
  Bright as a noontide beam:
I sought for wisdom. Thou didst make its taste
  (Which was as spice and honey from the south)
  Ashes and gall and wormwood in my mouth.
Was this the fruit I sought with so much haste?

  I had a love
  (This bitterest did prove);
A mystic light of joy on earth and sky;
  Strange fears and hopes; a rainbow tear and
      smile,
  A transient splendour for a little while,
Then—sudden darkness: Lord, Thou knowest why.

What have I left?
Of friend, aim, love, bereft;
Stripped bare of everything I counted dear.
   What friend have I like that I lost! what call
   To action? nay, what love?
                    Lord, I have all
And more beside, if only Thou art near.

                    Adeline Sergeant.

Over the Hillside.

Farewell! In dimmer distance
  I watch your figures glide,
Across the sunny moorland,
  And brown hillside.

Each momently uprising,
  Large, dark, against the sky;
Then, in the vacant moorland,
  Alone sit I.

Along the unknown country
  Where your last footsteps pass,
What beauty decks the heavens
  And clothes the grass!

Over the mountain shoulder
  What glories may unfold!
'Though I see but the mountain,
  Blank, bare, and cold;

And the white road, slow winding
  To where, each after each,
You slipped away—oh, whither?
  I cannot reach.

F 3

And if I call, what answers?
  Only 'twixt earth and sky.
Like wail of parting spirit.
  The curlews cry.

Yet sunny is the moorland,
  And soft the pleasant air,
And little flowers, like blessings,
  Grow everywhere.

While, over all, the mountain
  Stands, sombre, calm, and still,
Immutable and steadfast
  As the One Will;

Which, done on earth, in heaven,
  Eternally confessed
By men, and saints, and angels,
  Be ever blest!

Under Its infinite shadow,
  Safer than light of ours,
I'll sit me down a little
  And gather flowers.

Then I will rise and follow,
  Without one wish to stay,
The path ye all have taken—
  The appointed way.

Resignation.

To a quaint old fashion'd homestead,
  With its ivied towers,
Came a Lady in the spring-time,
  Came, when April's sudden showers,
Glancing through the fitful sunshine,
  Ran down rainbows into flowers;
And she said, "I would not murmur;
  God's will must be done;
So I've brought my two twin daughters,
  And come here to feel the sun!"

Living in that quiet hamlet
  Through three chequer'd years,
She was known in every cottage;
  And the poor tell, in their tears,
How her presence made them happy,
  And her words dispell'd their fears.
When she said, "O do not murmur!
  God's will must be done;
Take my alms, and ask His blessing,
  And go out and feel the sun!"

Once a widow met her walking
  Near the churchyard stile,
With a brow as free from sadness
  As her soul was free from guile.

And she whisper'd as she join'd her,
  "Lady, teach me how to smile."
And she answer'd, " Honest neighbour,
  God's will must be done;
And whene'er thy heart is drooping.
  Then come out and feel the sun !"

" For I tell thee, I have troubles:
  More than one," she saith;
" Have I seen the face of anguish,
  Heard its quick and catching breath?
Yea, three pictures in my parlour
  Are now sanctified by death."
" Yet," she saith, " I do not murmur:
  God's will must be done:
But I take my two twin daughters.
  And go out and feel the sun !"

In the rain two graves are greening,
  Greening day by day,
And young children, when they near them
  Playing, cease to play,
Lose their smiles and merry glances,
  And in silence steal away.
Yet she says, " I will not murmur:
  God's will must be done:
But I love the streaming starlight
  Better than the alter'd sun."

Never weeps she, now they've left her.
  Weeps not in her grief,
But she talks of shining angels.
  With a wild uncheck'd belief:

When all earthly hopes have failed us,
  Hopes of Heav'n still give relief.
And she says, " I will not murmur ;
  God's will has been done :
And, though *I* am left in darkness,
  They are somewhere in the sun !"

James Pritchett Begg.

The Aged and the Dying.

" 'Truly life is sweet, and a pleasant thing it is to behold the sun; but sweeter is the life beyond life, and more pleasant it is to behold the sun behind the sun."—*Joseph Cook*.

Would You be Young Again?

WOULD you be young again?
  So would not I.
One tear to memory given,
  Onward I'd hie.
Life's dark flood forded o'er,
  All but at rest on shore,
Say, would you plunge once more
  With home so nigh?

Where are those dear ones now?
  My joy and delight,
Dear and more dear, though now
  Hidden from sight.
Where they rejoice to be,
  That is the land for me,
Fly time, fly speedily,
  Come life and light.

Baroness Nairne.

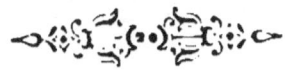

G

Wishes about Death.

I wish to have no wishes left,
   But to leave all to Thee:
And yet I wish that Thou should'st will
   Things that I wish should be.

And these two wills I feel within
   When on my death I muse;
But Lord! I have a death to *die*,
   And not a death to choose.

Why should I choose? for in Thy love,
   Most surely I descry
A gentler death than I myself
   Should dare to ask to die.

But Thou wilt not disdain to hear
   What these few wishes are,
Which I abandon to Thy love,
   And to Thy wiser care.

Triumphant death I would not ask,
   Rather would deprecate;
For dying souls deceive themselves
   Soonest when most elate.

All graces I would crave to have
  Calmly absorbed in one—
A perfect sorrow for my sins,
  And duties left undone.

I would the light of reason, Lord,
  Up to the last might shine,
That my own hands might hold my soul
  Until it passed to Thine.

And I would pass in silence, Lord,
  No brave words on my lips,
Lest pride should cloud my soul, and I
  Should die in the eclipse.

But when and where, and by what pain,—
  All this is one to me;
I only long for such a death
  As most shall honour Thee.

Long life dismays me, by the sense
  Of my own weakness scared;
And by Thy grace a sudden death
  Need not be unprepared.

One wish is hard to be unwished—
  That I at last might die
Of grief, for having wronged with sin
  Thy spotless Majesty.

F. W. Faber

"Having a Desire to Depart."

Eyes she had in whose dark lustre,
  Slumbered wild and mystic beams;
And a brow of polished marble,
  Pale abode of gorgeous dreams.
Dreams that caught the hues and splendours
  Which the radiant future shows,
For the past was nought but anguish,
  And a sepulchre of woes!
Therefore from its scenes and sorrows,
  All her heart and soul were riven,
And her thoughts kept ever wandering
  With the angels up to heaven.

When they told her of the pleasures.
  Which the future had in store,
When her sorrows would have faded,
  And her anguish would be o'er:
Told her of her wealth and beauty.
  And the triumphs in her train:
Told her of the many others.
  Who would sigh for her again.
She but caught one half their meaning,
  While the rest afar was driven,
"Yes," she murmur'd, "they are happy.
  They I mean who dwell in heaven"

When they wished once more to see her,
    Mingling with the bright and fair,
When they told her of the splendour,
    And the rank that would be there:
Told her that amid the glitter
    Of that brilliant living sea,
There was none so sought and sighed for,
    None so beautiful as she;
Still she heeded not the flattery,
    Heard but half the utterance given;
" Yes," she answer'd, " there are bright ones,
    Many too I know in heaven."

When they spoke of sunlit glories,
    Summer days and moonlit hours;
Told her of the spreading woodland,
    With its treasury of flowers;
Clustering fruits, and vales and mountains,
    Flower-banks mirror'd in clear springs,
Winds whose music ever mingled
    With the hum of glancing wings.
Scenes of earthly bliss and beauty
    Far from all her thought were driven,
And she fancied that they told her
    Of the happiness of heaven.

For one master-pang had broken
    The sweet spell of her young life,
And henceforth its calm and sunshine
    Were as tasteless as its strife;
Henceforth all its gloom and grandeur,
    All the music of its streams,
All its thousand pealing voices,
    Spoke the language of her dreams:

G 3

Dreams that wander'd on like orphans,
   From all earthly solace driven,
Searching for their great Protector,
   And the palace gates of heaven.

J. Stanyan Bigg.

In the June Twilight.

In the June twilight, in the soft grey twilight,
The yellow sun-glow trembling through the rainy
  eve,
As my love lay quiet came the solemn fiat,
"All these things *for ever, for ever*, thou must
  leave."

My love she sank down quivering, like a pine in
  tempest shivering,
" I have had so little happiness yet beneath the
  sun,
I have called the shadow sunshine, and the merest
  frosty moonshine,
I have, weeping, blessed the Lord for, as if daylight had begun.

" Till he sent a sudden angel, with a glorious sweet
  evangel,
Who turned all my tears to pearl gems, and
  crowned *me*—so little worth,
Me! and through the rainy even changed this poor
  earth into heaven,
Or, by wondrous revelation brought the heavens
  down to earth.

"O the strangeness of the feeling! O the infinite
    revealing,
To think how God must love me, to have made me
    so content,
Though I would have served him humbly, and
    patiently and dumbly,
Without any angel standing in the pathway that I
    went."

In the June twilight—in the lessening twilight,
My love cried from my bosom an exceeding bitter
    cry,
" Lord wait a little longer, until my soul is stronger,
Wait till Thou hast taught me to be content to die."

Then the tender face, all woman, took a glory
    super-human,
And she seemed to watch for something or see some
    I could not see,
From my arms she rose full statured, all trans-
    figured, queenly featured,
" As Thy will is done in heaven. so on earth still
    let it be."

    *   *   *   *   *   *

I go lonely, I go lonely, and I feel that earth is only
The vestibule of palaces whose courts we never
    win;
Yet I see my palace shining, where my love sits
    amaranths twining,
And I know the gates stand open, and I shall enter
    in.   *D. M. Craik.*

Passing Away.

Passing away, saith the world, passing away.
Chances, beauty and youth sapped day by day:
Thy life never continueth in one stay,
Is the eye waxen dim, is the dark hair changing
    to grey,
That hath won neither laurel nor bay?
I shall clothe myself in Spring and bud in May!
Thou, root-stricken, shalt not rebuild thy decay,
On my bosom for aye,
Then I answered: Yea.

Passing away. saith my soul, passing away;
With its burden of fear and hope, of labour and
    play,
Hearken what the past doth witness and say:
Rust in thy gold, a moth is in thine array.
A canker is in thy bud, thy leaf must decay,
At midnight, at cockcrow, at morning, one certain
    day,
Lo, the bridegroom shall come and shall not delay
Watch thou and pray,
Then I answered: Yea.

Passing away, saith my God, passing away
Winter passeth after the long delay;
New grapes on the vine, new figs on the tender
     spray,
Turtle calleth turtle in Heaven's May.
Though I tarry, wait for me, trust me, watch and
     pray,
Arise, come away, night is passed and lo it is day,
My love, my sister, my spouse, thou shalt hear me
     say,
Then I answered: Yea.

Christina G. Rosetti.

A Song of the River.

Many waters go softly dreaming
  On to the sea;
But the River of Death floweth softest
  By tower and tree.

By smiling village and meadow,
  In the morning light:
By palace gate and by cottage
  In the dim hush of night.

No sigh when the wistful moonlight
  Seeks that cold breast—
No smile when the gold of Sunset
  Burns in the west—

No rush of the mournful waters
  Breaks on the ear,
To tell us when life is strongest
  That death flows near.

But through throbbing hearts of cities,
  In the heat of the day,
The cool dark River passeth,
  On its silent way.

And where the Good Shepherd leadeth
  To pastures green,
Even the dark " still waters "
  Of death are seen.

This is the River that " follows "
  Where'er we go,}
No sand so dry and thirsty
  But these strange waters flow.

To fainting men in the desert
  No *living* streams appear :
But the waters of Death rise softly,
  Solemn and clear.

And down to the silent River,
  By night and day,
Old men and maidens wander ever,
  And pass away.

Some go with the voice of thanksgiving
  And melody,
And some in silence at midnight,
  When none are by.

Some go where the smiling meadows
  Sweep to the River-side,
And the pale sweet flowers are blowing.
  Close to the solemn tide.

And some are summoned at midnight,
  To cross in haste.
When the banks are steep and frowning.
  And the land lies waste.

No tender smiling of sunset,
   No pale death-flowers
Which can make the banks of the River sweet
   In dying hours;

Only a sudden leaping
   From the frowning height,
To the cold dark breast of the River—
   And then the silence of night.

Many waters go softly dreaming
   On to the sea,
But the River of Death floweth softest
   To thee and me.

We have trod the sands of the desert
   Under a burning sun;
Oh sweet will the touch of the waters be
   To feet whose journey is done!

Unto Him whose love has washed us
   Whiter than snow,
We shall pass through the shallow River
   With hearts aglow.

For the Lord's voice on the Waters
   Lingereth sweet:
" He that *is* washed needeth only
   To wash his feet."

                         B. M.

"Wind Me a Summer Crown,"
she said.

"Wind me a Summer Crown," she said,
  "And set it on my brows;
For I must go while I am young
  Home to my Father's house.

"And make me ready for the day,
  And let me not be stayed;
I would not linger on the way
  As if I was afraid.

"O! will the golden courts of heaven,
  When I have paced them o'er,
Be lovely as my lily walks,
  Which I must see no more?

"And will the seraph hymns and harps,
  When they have filled my ear,
Be tender as my mother's voice
  Which I must never hear?"

Your mother's tones shall reach you still,
  Even sweeter than they were,
And the false love that broke your heart
  Shall be forgotten there.

And not of star or flower is born
  The beauty of that shore,
There is a Face which you shall see,
  And wish for nothing more.

Menella Bute Smedley.

Paradise.

It's, oh, in Paradise that I fain would be,
Away from earth and weariness, and all beside:
Earth is too full of loss with its dividing sea,
But Paradise upbuilds the bower for the bride.

Where flowers are yet in bud, while the boughs are
    green,
I would get quit of earth, and get robed for heaven
Putting on my raiment white within the screen,
Putting on my crown of gold whose gems are seven.

Fair is the fourfold river that maketh no moan,
Fair are the trees, fruit-bearing of the wood,
Fair are the gold and bdellium and the onyx stone,
And I know the gold of that land is good.

O my love, my dove, lift up your eyes
Toward the eastern gate like an opening rose.
You and I who parted will meet in Paradise,
Pass within and sing when the gates unclose.

This life is but the passage of a day,
This life is but a pang and all is over,
But in the life to come which fades not away
Every love shall abide and every lover.

He who wore out pleasure and mastered all ove,
Solomon, wrote " Vanity of vanities,"
Down to death, of all that went before.
In his mighty long life the record is this.

With loves by the hundred, wealth beyond measure
Is this he who wrote " vanity of vanities !"
Yea " Vanity of vanities " he saith of pleasure,
And of all he learned set his seal to this.

Yet we love and faint not, for our love is one,
And we hope and flag not, for our hope is sure.
Although there be nothing new beneath the Sun
And no help for life, and for death no cure.

The road to death is life, the gate of life is death,
We who wake shall sleep, we shall wax who wane
Let us not vex our souls for stoppage of a breath,
The fall of a river that turneth not again.

Be the road short and be the gate near,—
Shall a short road tire, a strait gate appal?
The loves that meet in Paradise shall cast out fear
And Paradise hath room for you, and me, and all.

Christina G. Rossetti.

Dominus Illuminatio Mea.

In the hour of death, after this life's whim,
When the heart beats low, and the eyes grow dim,
And pain has exhausted every limb—
    The lover of the Lord shall trust in Him.

When the will has forgotten the lifelong aim,
And the mind can only disgrace its fame,
And man is uncertain of his own name—
    The power of the Lord shall fill this frame.

When the last sigh is heaved, and the last tear shed,
And the coffin is waiting beside the bed,
And the widow and child forsake the dead—
    The angel of the Lord shall lift this head.

For even the purest delight may pall,
The power must fail, and the pride must fall,
And the love of the dearest friends grow small—
    But the glory of the Lord is all in all

                  R. D. B.

"I will lift up mine eyes unto the hills."

I am pale with sick desire
For my heart is far away
From this world's fitful fire
And this world's waning day;
In a dream it overleaps
A world of tedious ills
To where the sunshine sleeps
On the everlasting hills.
Say the saints: There angels ease us
Glorified and white.
They say: We rest in Jesus
Where is not day or night.

My soul saith; I have sought
For a home that is not gained,
I have spent yet nothing bought,
Have laboured but not attained;
My pride strove to mount and grow
And hath not dwindled down ;
My love sought love, and lo!
Hath not attained its crown.
Say the saints: Fresh souls increase us
None languish or recede.
They say: We love our Jesus,
And he loves us in deed

I cannot rise above,
I cannot rest beneath.
I cannot find out love,
Or escape from death.
Dear hopes and joys gone by
Still mock me with a name;
My best beloved die,
And I cannot die with them.
Say the saints: No deaths decrease us
Where our joy is glorious.
They say: We live in Jesus
Who once died for us.

O my soul, she beats her wings
And pants to fly away
Up to immortal things
In the heavenly day.
Yet she flags and almost faints;
Can such be meant for me?
Come and see, say the saints.
Saith Jesus, Come and see.
Say the saints: His pleasures please us
Before God and the Lamb.
Come and taste my sweets, saith Jesus:
Be with me where I am.

Christina G. Rossetti

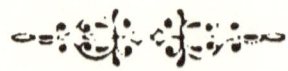

Through the Gates.

Good-bye, ah, good-bye; you are going
　　To enter the Silent Land,
And your life is vanishing from me,
　　Though fast I hold your hand.
Your head on my bosom will lie, love,
　　Clasp'd in a close embrace,
But where will your soul be wandering.
　　When your breath fails off my face?

The Silent Land! Hark, how music
　　Thrills through the sweeten'd air,
It is surely sounding from heaven,
　　Unknown to us otherwhere.
A far-off journey! kind angels
　　Stand reaching to me their hand.
It is but a step and a step-lift,
　　From the earth on which you stand.

Is the parting, then, so complete, love?
　　Perhaps you may come again,
And give me some word or token
　　That you, though chang'd, are the same.
A whisper in evening stillness,
　　A vision in broad, bright day,
A touch as of long-trail'd garments,
　　Soft-touching and floating away.

I know not.   But bid me good-bye now,
  As going at night to my room,
If I may I will open the door, love,
  And call to you out of the gloom.
If I may not, the Lord is our keeper,
  And we are still in His care;
You on earth, I in heaven—both guarded,
  Both safe, till you follow me there.

Alfred Norris.

A Good Confession.

[Suggested by hearing of a tombstone in a country churchyard in Wales, on which was inscribed the name of a man who had lived some years above eighty, yet was said to be (alluding to his conversion to Christ) only "four years old when he died."]

If you ask me how long I have been in the world,
    I'm old, I'm very old ;
If you ask me how many years I've lived, it'll very
    soon be told.
Past eighty years of age, yet only four years old !

Eighty years and more astray upon the mountains
    high.
In a land that's full of pits and snares, and that's
    desolate and dry.
I've oft been weary, oft been cold, and oft been like
    to die;

And there I'd have wandered, wandered still, as I
    wandered many a day :
I'd lose the track-marks of the flock, I'd got so far
    away
If Jesus had not met me, that seeks for them that
    stray.

The Shepherd took me in His arms, for you see I'm
    getting old,
And my strength is, as the Psalmist says, gone like
    a tale that's told;
" And other sheep," the Shepherd says, " I have,
    and to the fold

Them also must I bring," for He has many little
    lambs,
All milk-white, mild, and innocent, a-skipping by
    their dams;
And many sheep that have been driven along the
    dusty roads,
Hard driven along by dogs and men, and pricked
    with iron goads,

And marked with iron brands to show they've oft
    been bought and sold;
Brown ragged sheep, with fleeces torn, and faces
    wizened and old;

And if you ask me which of these I think He loves
    the best—
The lambs or sheep—I cannot say: He'll love me
    with the rest.
For " Feed my little lambs," He said, when He gave
    His flock to keep,
To Peter, once and twice He said to Peter, " Feed
    my sheep."

He's got a garden full of flowers, all planted row by
    row,
Roses and pinks and mignonette a-coming into blow,
And many little pleasant herbs that near each other
    grow:

Balm o' Gilead, mint and thyme, and sage and
  marjorie,
And many a dry old stick and stalk, and many a
  withered tree,
That's neither good for use nor show, and these
  are folks like me;

And many such-like ones He's got, but scripture
  sayeth " Lo!
He taketh such and maketh them to flourish and to
  grow."
For He's not a man that He should judge by seeing
  of His eyes,
He's not a son of man that He should any one
  despise,
He's God Himself and far too kind for that, and
  far too wise.

He's God Himself come down from Heaven to
  raise us when we fall;
He's come to heal us when we're sick, to hear us
  when we call:
If He hadn't come to do us good, He wouldn't
  have come at all.

And " Ask, He says, and I will give, and knock and
  I to you
Will open," Jesus says to us, and I know that it is
  true,
It isn't Him would say the things He doesn't mean
  to do.

I

He didn't come to judge the world, He didn't come
    to blame,
He didn't only come to seek, it was to save He
    came,
And when we call Him Saviour, then we call Him
    by His name.

He sought for me when I was lost, He brought me
    to His fold,
He doesn't look for much from me, for He doesn't
    need be told
I'm past eighty years of age, and yet but four years
    old.

Dora Greenwell.

Vespers.

When I have said my quiet say,
When I have sung my little song,
How sweetly, sweetly dies the day,
The valley and the hills along;
How sweet the summons, "Come away,"
That calls me from the busy throng!

I thought beside the water's flow
Awhile to lie beneath the leaves,
I thought in autumn's harvest glow
To rest my head upon the sheaves:
But, lo! methinks the day was brief
And cloudy; flower, nor fruit, nor leaf
I bring, and yet accepted, free,
And blest, my Lord, I come to Thee.

What matter now for promise lost,
Though blast of Spring or Summer rain
For broken hopes and wasted pains
What if the olive little yield,
What if the grape be blighted.   Thine
The corn upon a thousand fields,
Upon a thousand hills the vine.

Thou lovest still the poor: oh, blest
In poverty beloved to be
Less lowly is my choice confess'd,
I love the best in loving Thee!
My spirit bare before Thee stands,
I bring no gift, I ask no sign,
I come to Thee with empty hands
The surer to be filled from Thine!

Dora Greenwell.

A Prayer.

I would not ask Thee that my days
  Should flow quite smoothly on and on ;
Lest I should learn to love the world
  Too well, ere all my time was done.

I would not ask Thee that my work
  Should never bring me pain nor fear,
Lest I should learn to work alone,
  And never wish Thy presence near.

I would not ask Thee that my friends
  Should always kind and constant be ;
Lest I should learn to lay my faith,
  In them alone and not in Thee.

But I would ask Thee still to give,
  By night my sleep—by day my bread,
And that the counsel of Thy Word,
  Should shine and show the path to tread.

And I would ask a humble heart,
  A changeless will to work and wake,
A firm faith in Thy Providence,
  The rest—'tis Thine to give or take.

Alfred Norris.

BY THE EDITOR.

———o———

CALLS TO CHRIST. By Rev. W. R.
NICOLL. Second Edition. Fifth Thousand.

" Force and freshness are eminently the charac-
teristics of these discourses."—*C. H. Spurgeon in*
" *Sword and Trowel.*"

"Marked by freshness, earnestness and striking
directness of force."—*Rev. Dr Maclaren, Man-
chester.*

" A model of Christian expostulation and pleading."—*Rev. Dr Parker in the* " *Fountain.*"

"It is a new voice that is pleading with an in
tonation and melody of its own."—*Daily Review.*

"Ought to be in the hands of every one who
attempts to preach the gospel."—*Christian.*